First published in 2014 by Scholastic Children's Books
Euston House, 24 Eversholt Street, London NW1 1DB
a division of Scholastic Ltd
www.scholastic.co.uk
London ~ New York ~ Toronto ~ Sydney ~ Auckland
Mexico City ~ New Delhi ~ Hong Kong

Text copyright © 2014 Claire Freedman
Illustrations copyright © 2014 Russell Julian
HB ISBN 978 1407 13788 9
PB ISBN 978 1407 13789 6

The moral rights of Claire Freedman
and Russell Julian have been asserted.

Papers used by Scholastic Children's Books
are made from wood grown in sustainable forests.

For Theo Henry John James
C.F.
For Peter Moruzzi
R.J.

GEORGE's DRagON
at the
Fire station

George's pet dragon, Sparky, was snoring loudly!
"Wake up, Sparky!" called George. "Today is the open day at the fire station. We don't want to miss it!"

Fire
Station
Open
Day

"SNORT...!"
squeaked Sparky excitedly.
He leapt up and sent the
alarm clock flying!

"Wakey-shakey!"
he gasped.

"I suppose even Sparky should be safe at a fire station," joked Mum, as Sparky gulped down his breakfast and accidentally burned another hole in her tablecloth.

"Of course he will – won't you Sparky?" smiled George.
Sparky nodded happily and knocked over George's dad's cereal.

At the fire station, Firefighter Lottie and
Firefighter Fred were showing everyone around.

Wheeee!

Lots of children were having fun
sliding down the fireman's pole.

"Zippy-fun-doodah!"
laughed Sparky, rushing up to have a go.
"No Sparky, stop!" cried George.
"You're too big."
But it was too late...

Sparky's bottom was stuck fast.

George pushed one end.
Firefighter Fred pulled the other.
"Gotta-botty-biggy!"
gulped Sparky.

WHUUUMP!

Sparky shot free at last.

"But now **I'm** stuck!" gasped Firefighter Fred.

It was the fire
demonstration next.
  "You will behave, won't you
Sparky?" said George.
Sparky waved his tail excitedly
and sent a sand bucket flying!
Luckily, Dad was wearing
a safety helmet!

Helmets
on!

"Right!" announced Firefighter Lottie. "In this room we set fire to things and then practise putting out the flames! Today we are going to safely set fire to that box."

"It's getting very smoky in here," coughed George.
"Sniffle-wiffle-tickle!" said Sparky.
His nose was feeling very prickly.
Sparky sniffed a huge snuffly snort.

SWOOOSH!

Oh no! A giant flame shot out from his snout.

SIZZLE!

Now the teeny-weeny fire was a big blaze!
"Sparky!" cried George.
"Ooopsa-shamey-flamey!"
squeaked Sparky in embarrassment.

"Don't worry – I'll soon put the fire out!"
Firefighter Lottie said.
Quickly, she unravelled the long water hose.
   "Stand back everyone!" she warned.
"You don't want to get wet!"
   Firefighter Lottie turned the big red water wheel to 'on'.

Everyone held their breath and watched.

"That's strange..." frowned Firefighter Fred, peering down the hose. "Why isn't any water coming out?"

"Sparky!" whispered George. "You're standing on the hose pipe!"

SPLOOOOOSH!

There was plenty of water coming out now!

"Droppy-soppy!" blushed Sparky.

"We're soaked!" said Firefighter Fred crossly.
"If Sparky can't behave, he must go home!"

Poor George – he felt SO disappointed. But just then...

DING DING! DING DING!

The fire alarm bell rang loudly. It was a REAL emergency! "Actions stations! We've had a 999 call!" shouted Firefighter Lottie. "Mrs Trimble's kitten, Fluffy, is stuck up a tall tree. We need to rescue it!"

"Wow!" gasped the children excitedly.

Neee naaar! Neeee naaar!

Off the fire engine sped, blue lights flashing.

Everyone followed to see what would happen!

FIRE 2

"Ooooh!" the children gulped. Fluffy WAS in trouble.

"Aaaah!" they cried, as Firefighter Fred was lifted high up to reach the kitten. But Fluffy was too scared to let go of the branch!

"How will we get poor Fluffy down?" wailed Mrs Trimble.

George looked at Sparky. Sparky looked at George.

"Sparky can help!" cried George.

"Hmmm..." said Firefighter Lottie doubtfully.

Suddenly...

CRA-AAA-CK!

"Oh no!" gasped the crowd.
"The branch is breaking!"
"Quick, Sparky – before
Fluffy falls!" cried George.

SNAP!

"MIAOW!"

WHEEEE! Up Sparky flew.
"Savey-wavey!"
said Sparky, gently catching Fluffy mid-air.

"Hooray!" the children cheered.

"Thank you!" smiled Mrs Trimble happily.

"Well done, Sparky!" grinned the firefighters.

George was SO proud of his pet dragon.

After that, everyone enjoyed the rest of the open day. Sparky did accidentally burn a ladder – but fortunately Firefighter Lottie had reached the bottom just in time!

As a big thank you for saving Fluffy, Sparky and George
were given their **very own** fire-fighting kit.
The fire extinguisher was brilliant — as it came in handy on the way
home!